For St. John's Singers. "Happiness is those who sing with you." —J.R.A.

To young dancers and dreamers everywhere —J.S.

Text copyright © 2022 by John Robert Allman
Jacket art and interior illustrations copyright © 2022 by Julianna Swaney

All rights reserved. Published in the United States by Doubleday, an imprint of Random House Children's Books, a division of Penguin Random House LLC, New York.

Doubleday is a registered trademark and the Doubleday colophon is a trademark of Penguin Random House LLC.

American Ballet Theatre, ABT, America's National Ballet Company, and the ABT Logo are registered trademarks of Ballet Theatre Foundation, Inc., dba American Ballet Theatre. www.abt.org

Grateful acknowledgment is made to Richard Hudson for permission to print costume design illustrations on pages 36–37, copyright © Richard Hudson. Used by permission of Richard Hudson. All rights reserved.

Visit us on the Web! rhcbooks.com
Educators and librarians, for a variety of teaching tools, visit us at RHTeachersLibrarians.com

*Library of Congress Cataloging-in-Publication Data*
Names: Allman, John Robert, author. | American Ballet Theatre. | Swaney, Julianna, illustrator.
Title: The night before The Nutcracker / by John Robert Allman ; illustrated by Julianna Swaney.
Description: First edition. | New York : Doubleday Books for Young Readers, 2022. | Audience: Ages 3–7.
Summary: "A behind-the-scenes peek at all the hard work, creativity, and excitement that lead up to the opening night performance of American Ballet Theatre's The Nutcracker" —Provided by publisher.
Identifiers: LCCN 2021047670 (print) | LCCN 2021047671 (ebook) |
ISBN 978-0-593-18091-4 (hardcover) | ISBN 978-0-593-18092-1 (library binding) |
ISBN 978-0-593-18117-1 (ebook)
Subjects: CYAC: Stories in rhyme. | Ballet—Fiction. | Nutcracker (Choreographic work)—Fiction.
Classification: LCC PZ8.3.A443 Ni 2022 (print) | LCC PZ8.3.A443 (ebook) | DDC [E]—dc23

MANUFACTURED IN CHINA
10 9 8 7 6 5 4 3 2 1
First Edition

AMERICAN BALLET THEATRE
*presents*

# The Night Before The Nutcracker

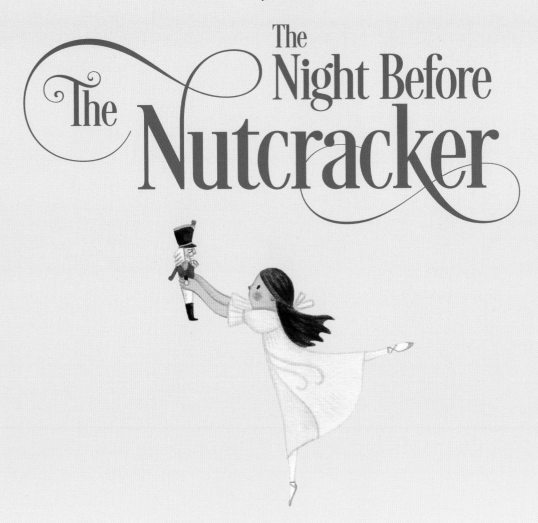

## By John Robert Allman
## Illustrations by Julianna Swaney

Doubleday Books for Young Readers

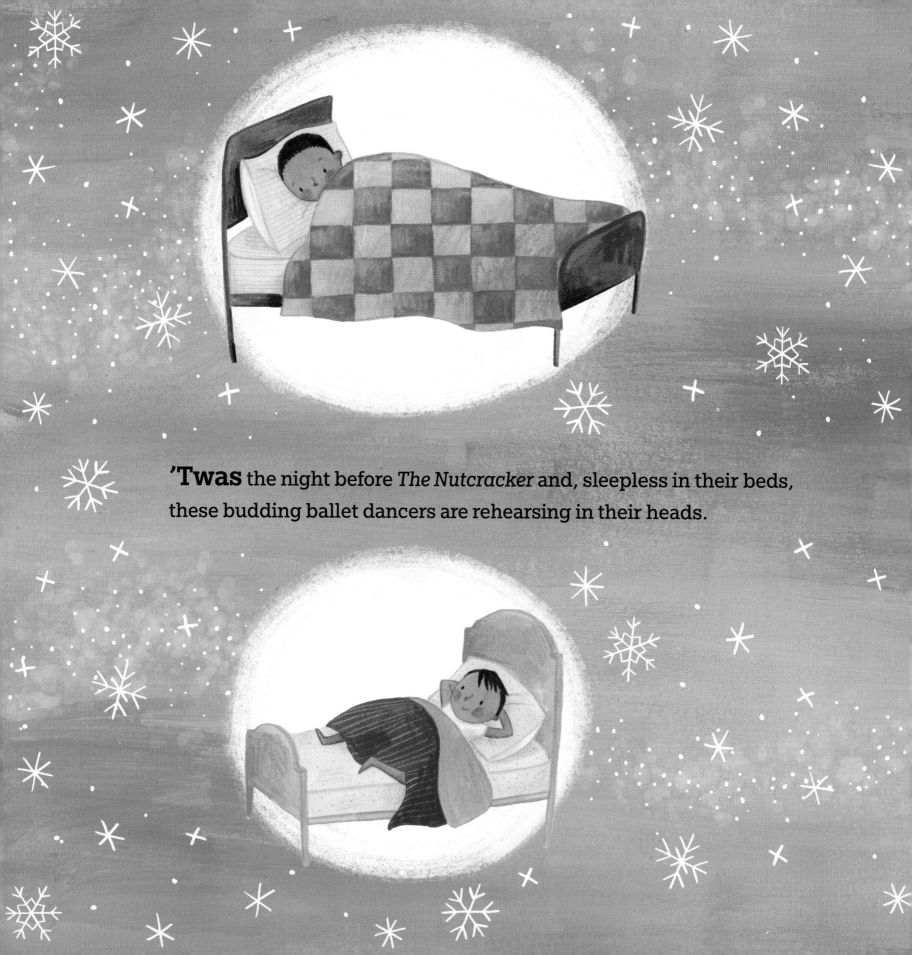

'**Twas** the night before *The Nutcracker* and, sleepless in their beds, these budding ballet dancers are rehearsing in their heads.

After months and months of making sure that every move is right,
it's the moment they've been working for: Tomorrow's opening night!

They dazzled their directors
with astonishing auditions,
full of energetic pirouettes
and elegant positions.

From hopefuls by the hundred,
it's the fortunate and few
who are cast as classic characters
from 1892.

Precision in performance
comes with passion and with prep,
so they practice every pantomime
and study every step.

As soon as students shine
in every picture-perfect pose,
they are ready for rehearsals
and for run-throughs with the pros.

Each costume, made to measure, is exquisitely constructed . . .

. . . and the orchestra below is tuning up to be conducted.

On stage for dress rehearsal,
sets and lights are bold and bright,
and applause awaits tomorrow
when, at last, it's opening night!

They'll shuffle through the stage door,
and they'll warm up at the barre.
Then it's costumes, hair, and makeup
for each fearless future star.

There's time to spare for schoolwork and for lucky last embraces
till the burst of joy and jitters when a stagehand hollers, "Places!"

Tchaikovsky's music sets a mood of jolly jubilation
as Clara and her brother host a Christmas celebration.

While merrymakers mingle, Clara skips and spins with joy
when Drosselmeyer offers her the ballet's fabled toy.

She sneaks downstairs much later, and she sees, to her surprise,
her soldier and his squadron spring to life before her eyes.

Triumphantly,
the troopers overcome
the Mouse King's swarm
as the shocked and sleepy Clara
sees her Nutcracker transform.

A swift and steady snowfall stalls the couple's getaway
until Drosselmeyer saves them with a send-off in his sleigh.

In the wings at intermission,
Mother Ginger's kids are stowed
while behind the scenes, the crew is sweeping
snowflakes by the load.

BARRES

The second act transports us to the lavish Land of Sweets
for a friendly fairy's festival of wondrous worldly treats.

From far and near,
her revelers inspire and impress,
and a cavalcade of clowns
pops out of Mother Ginger's dress.

Finally, a pas de deux
that Clara won't forget:
She's transformed into a princess
for a dashing dream duet.

Suddenly, she wakes at home, and nothing's as it seems.
In disbelief, she wonders, "Was it only in my dreams?"

The ballet ends and, smiling smiles as sweet as sugarplums,
the cast will bow, the crowd will cheer, and down the curtain comes.

Their families and their friends await with oohs and aahs and flowers
at a post-performance party where they'll celebrate for hours . . .

. . . but not too late, for though they've danced through *one* successful show, they'll be back again tomorrow and have many more to go!

With months of work behind them, now they're dreaming with delight of the magic and the merriment to come tomorrow night.

# AMERICAN BALLET THEATRE's
## *The Nutcracker*

**The story, featuring original costume illustrations by Richard Hudson**

ABT world premiere: December 23, 2010, Brooklyn Academy of Music, New York
Music by Pyotr Ilyich Tchaikovsky • Choreography by Alexei Ratmansky •
Scenery and costumes by Richard Hudson • Lighting by Jennifer Tipton

**ACT 1, SCENE 1, THE KITCHEN:**
Meet the Stahlbaum children, Clara and Fritz, amid the busy preparation for their family's holiday party. With the work done, everyone heads to the parlor—but a hungry group of mice appear and pick at the food.

**ACT 1, SCENE 2, THE PARTY:**
Guests arrive for the big event. Clara's godfather, Drosselmeyer, gives her the Nutcracker, a doll he has made. Jealous Fritz spoils the fun by taking the Nutcracker and breaking it. Drosselmeyer fixes it, and the party eventually winds down before the family goes to bed.

### ACT 1, SCENE 3, THE BATTLE:

Clara sneaks downstairs to see her Nutcracker. Mice scamper in and steal her treasured gift, leading Clara to faint. She awakes to find a grand battle: the Mouse King and other mice versus the Nutcracker, who has come to life, and a troop of toy soldiers. Clara ends the fight by knocking out the Mouse King with her shoe, and the mice flee. As Clara looks over the wounded Nutcracker, he is magically transformed into a prince.

### ACT 1, SCENE 4, THE SNOW:

A blizzard sets in, and Clara and the prince are surrounded by dancing snowflakes. Drosselmeyer arrives to rescue them in a sleigh.

### ACT 2, LAND OF THE SUGAR PLUM FAIRY:

Drosselmeyer delivers Clara and the prince safely to the Land of the Sugar Plum Fairy, and a celebration is held. Clara and the prince are treated to a festival featuring performers from around the world and the comical Mother Ginger, who hides her many clownlike children—called Polichinelles—under her enormous dress. The gathering closes with a special waltz of flowers and bumblebees. At the end of an enchanted day, Clara sees a vision of her future in which she is a princess and dances with her Nutcracker prince.

### EPILOGUE, CHRISTMAS MORNING:

Clara awakes at home in her bed. As the kindhearted Drosselmeyer looks in through a window, Clara is reunited with her cherished Nutcracker doll, which was under her pillow. Have all her adventures been a dream?